MEG in the JUNGLE

Jan Pieńkowski
and David Walser

PUFFIN BOOKS

They fly all night

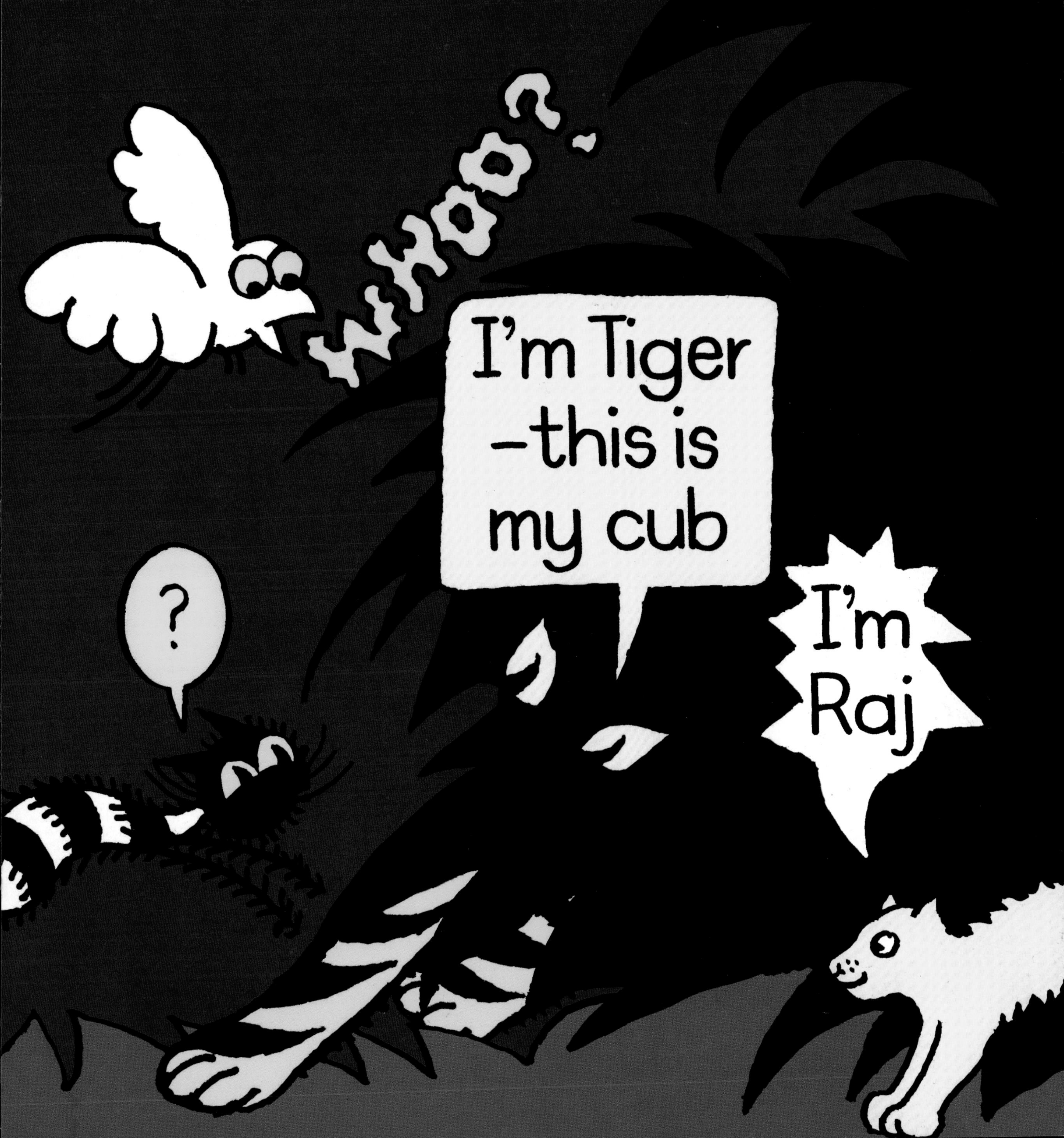
WHOO?
I'm Tiger
–this is
my cub
?
I'm
Raj

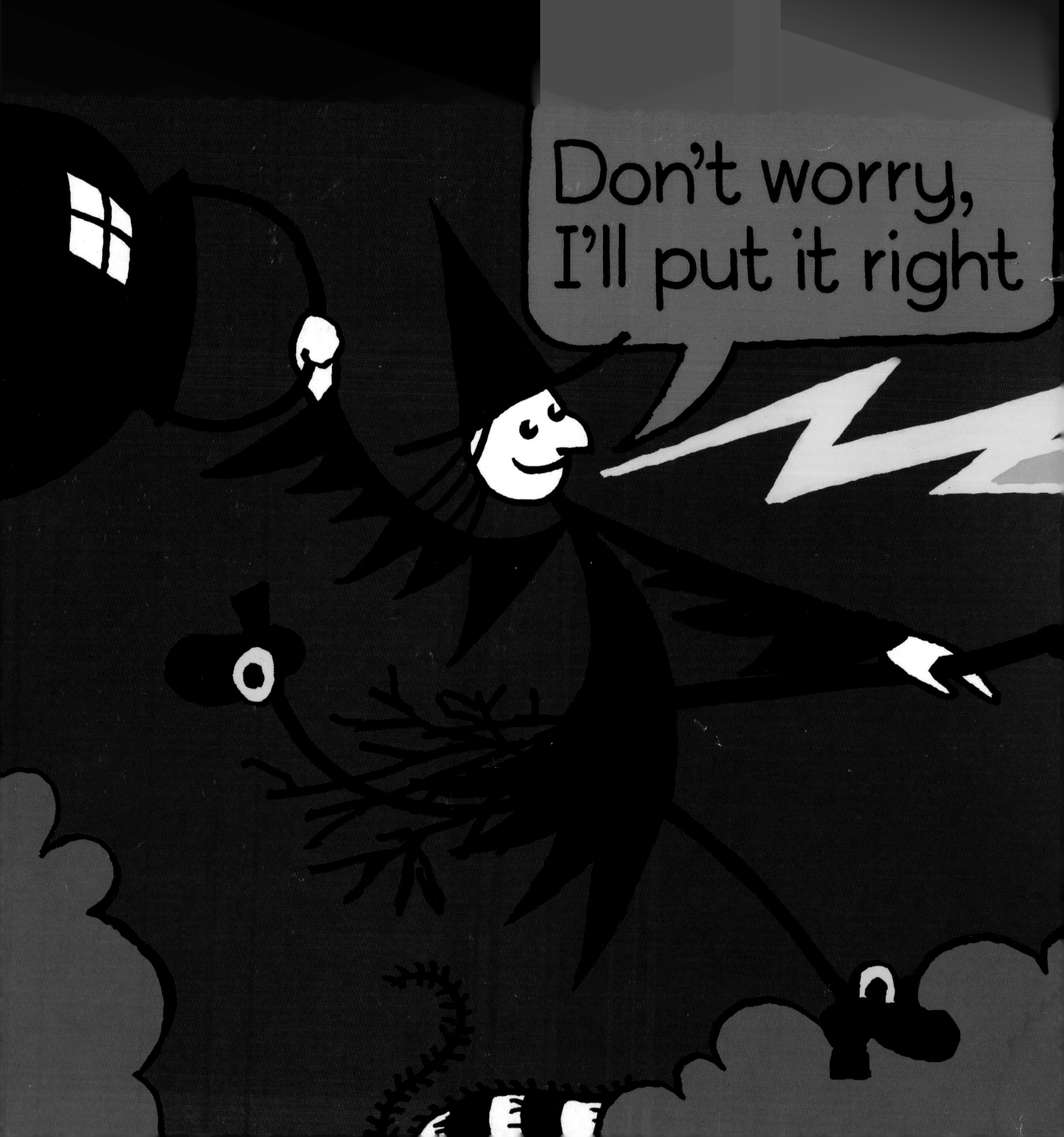
Don't worry,
I'll put it right

Pot of paint
And brushes four
Paint a stripe –
Then some more

Everyone brings a birthday present for Mog

Goodbye!